Grandude's Green Submarine

Dear Reader,

Do you like adventures?

My name is Edward Marshall Senior. But my grandchildren call me Grandude, and they are my Chillers – Lucy, Tom, Em and Bob. We love to go on magical adventures together. And this is the story of our journey to find another very special adventurer – why don't you come along for the ride!

Yours sincerely,

Grandude

To my own chillers with love – P.M.

For my family – K.D.

PUFFIN BOOKS

UK | USA | Canada | Ireland | Australia | India | New Zealand | South Africa

Puffin Books is part of the Penguin Random House group of companies whose addresses can be found at global.penguinrandomhouse.com.

Penguin
Random House
UK

First published 2021
001

Copyright © MPL Communications Ltd, 2021
Written by Paul McCartney
Illustrations by Kathryn Durst
The moral right of the author has been asserted

Printed in China
A CIP catalogue record for this book is available from the British Library
ISBN: 978–0–241–47293–4

All correspondence to: Puffin Books, Penguin Random House Children's,
One Embassy Gardens, 8 Viaduct Gardens, London SW11 7BW

Grandude's Green Submarine

Written by
Paul McCartney

Illustrated by
Kathryn Durst

PUFFIN

It was a BOILING hot summer's day.

Em

Lucy

"TOO HOT!" said Tom.

Tom

Bob

And the other Chillers – Lucy, Em and Bob – all agreed.

Grandude peeped out from his garden shed.
"Too hot for you, is it? Come inside."

'Welcome to my top-secret Inventions Shed!'
said Grandude.

It was as cool as an iced drink (or an ice rink)
– full of unusual cooling devices. And all
sorts of other mysterious creations, too.

As the Chillers explored, Lucy spotted a picture of Nandude, their adventurous grandmother.

Grandude's eyes sparkled. "I think she loves adventures even more than I do!"

"When will we see her again?" asked Bob.

"Perhaps *we* could go on an adventure to find her!" said Em.

"Great minds think alike," said Grandude.
"And I have a plan . . .

Follow me!"

Grandude led the children down a secret
passageway until they reached a locked door.

"This is my favourite invention yet," Grandude said,
opening the door to reveal . . .

A bright **green submarine!**

"What a beauty!" said Grandude.

As they all climbed aboard, Grandude took out his golden magic compass from his trouser pocket.

"We'll need a bit of magic to get started. This is no ordinary sub, you know!"

Magic needle spinning 'round, lift this green sub off the ground.

With a **Zing, bang, Sizzle,** the green submarine jerked and jolted, then sprang up into the air and shot through the roof of the shed!

The Chillers laughed and cheered as they zoomed up into the clouds.

"We're swimming through the sky," said Em.

"I think I know who might be able to help us find Nandude," said Grandude, as they flew along, singing songs and watching the world far below.

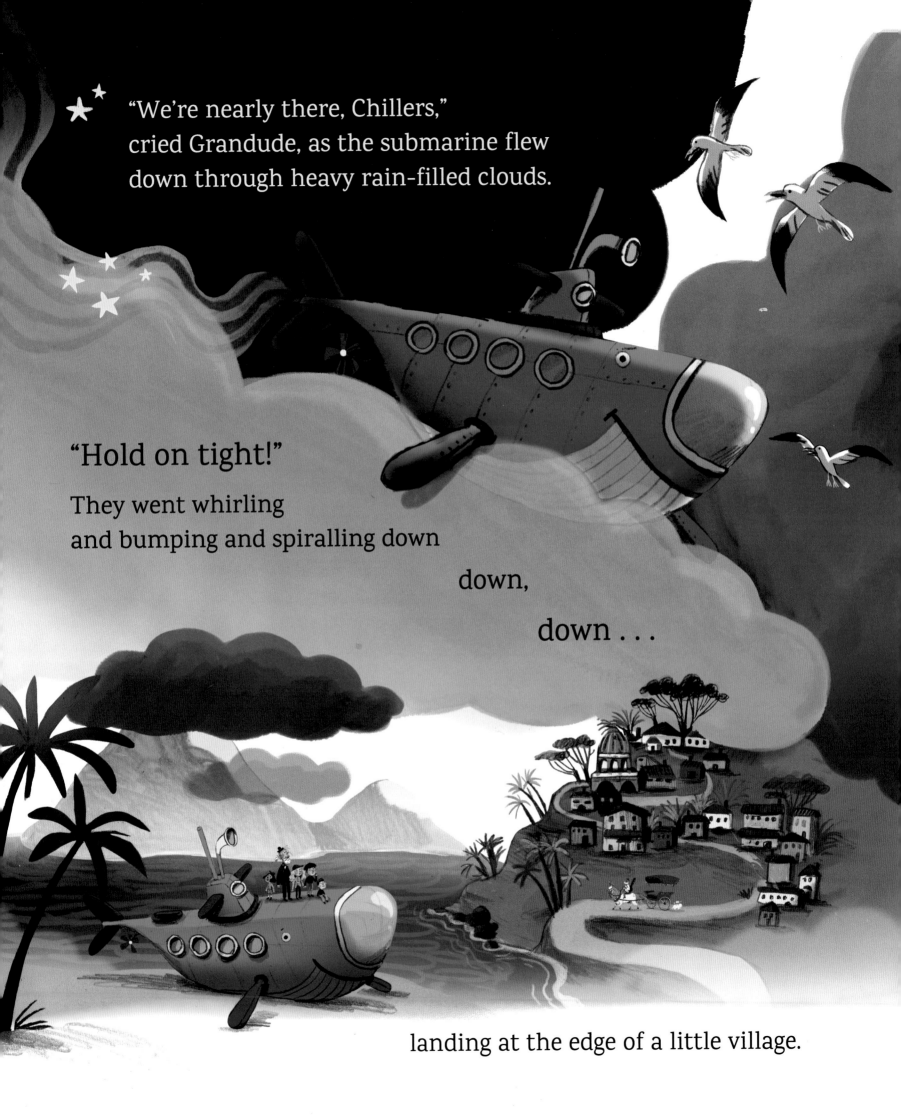

"We're nearly there, Chillers," cried Grandude, as the submarine flew down through heavy rain-filled clouds.

"Hold on tight!"

They went whirling and bumping and spiralling down

down,

down . . .

landing at the edge of a little village.

"Hey, Grandude!" shouted a man on a big white stallion, smiling and waving furiously.

"We're just where we need to be," said Grandude. "Meet my friend, Ravi."

"And you're just in time for the parade," said Ravi.

Ravi took Grandude and the Chillers to a shady terrace. It was the perfect spot to watch the parade, while Grandude and Ravi told stories about Nandude's adventures.

"Nandude taught me this tune," said Ravi, strumming his sitar. "If you want to find her, just follow the notes. And watch how it makes the animals sing and dance!"

But as they listened, another sound started.

Drip, drop, plip, plop — the rain had come.

"Oh no!" said Bob. "The storm has found us!"

"We won't be able to fly through a **monsoon!**"
said Tom as the rain poured down.

"Don't worry," said Grandude. "We won't need to fly.
Quick, Chillers! **Catch that sub!**"

The green submarine was floating
away on the rising rainwater!

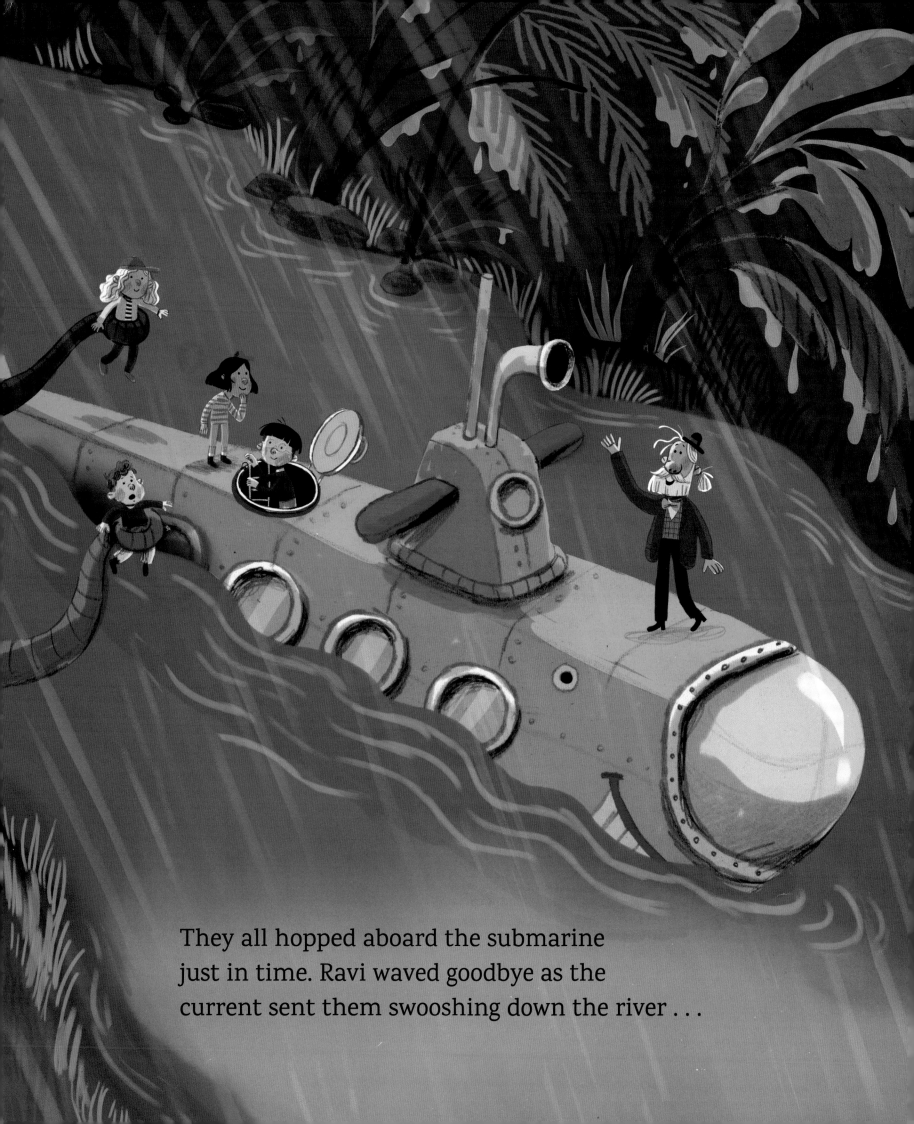

They all hopped aboard the submarine
just in time. Ravi waved goodbye as the
current sent them swooshing down the river . . .

"Where is the river taking us, Grandude?" asked Lucy.

"I have a **notion** we're heading for the **ocean!**" said Grandude.

As the river rushed them through a lush jungle, they heard a familiar tune . . .

The animals on the riverside were all singing snatches
of Nandude's song!

They passed **tigers** and **toucans**,

and **birds** and **baboons**,

leopards and **lemurs**,

warthogs and **bullfrogs**.

"If we follow the music, we're sure to find her!" said Bob.
The river widened and they reached its mouth . . .

And then the green submarine began to dive down

deep

deep

deep

into the shimmering blue ocean.

Deeper and deeper they went,
cruising past the most spectacular sea life.

Grandude happily pointed out dolphins, sharks
and whales, who all seemed excited to see him.

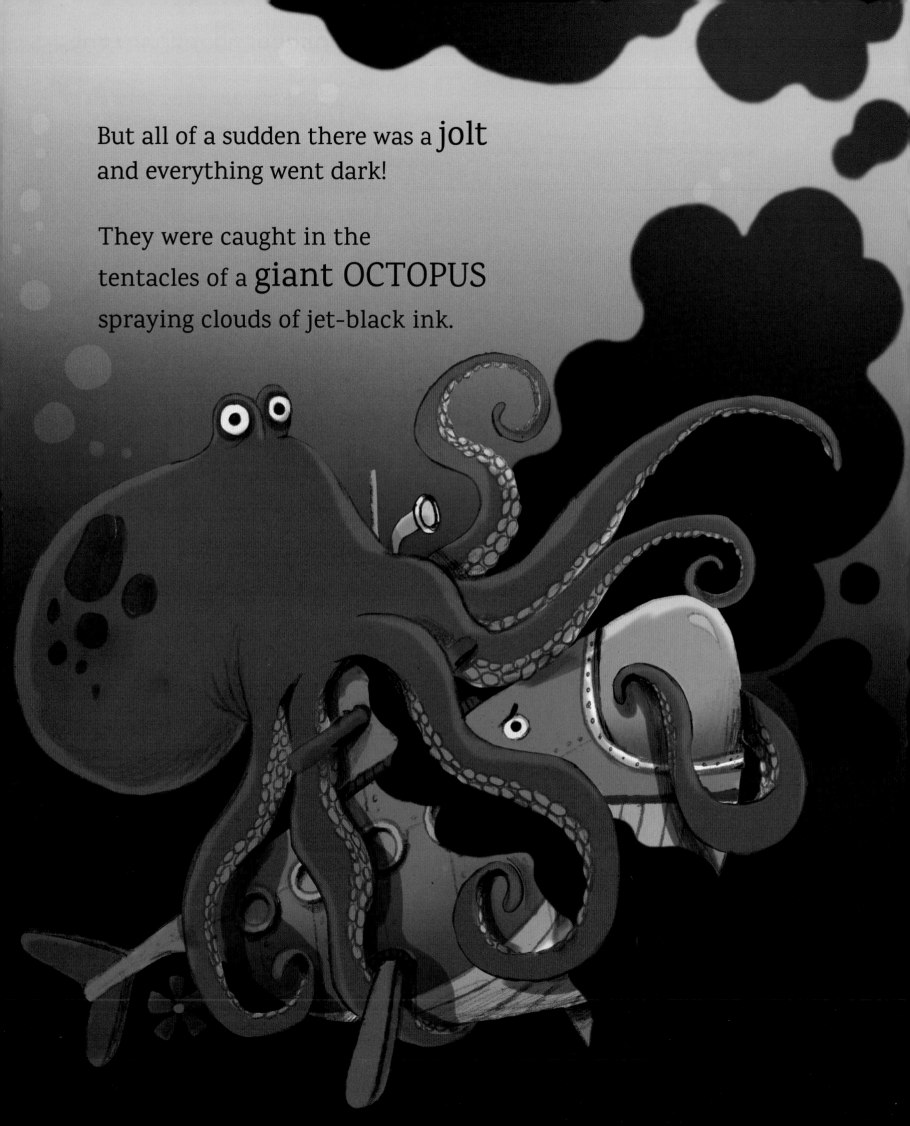

But all of a sudden there was a jolt
and everything went dark!

They were caught in the
tentacles of a giant OCTOPUS
spraying clouds of jet-black ink.

It was so dark that Grandude couldn't find his magic compass –
and even he was getting a little bit worried.

"What's that sound?" asked Bob nervously.

"It's that tune
we heard before –
Nandude's MUSIC!
And it's getting louder."
said Grandude.

Louder . . .
        and BRIGHTER!

Each note lit up the sea
in a magical light show.

It was Nandude!

Her huge underwater ship was sailing towards them.

As the ship approached, the octopus began to dance.
And as it danced, it let go of the green submarine.
Grandude and the Chillers were free!

Other sea creatures joined the octopus's wild dance.

And meanwhile a trail of magical music from
Nandude's ship scooped up the green submarine . . .

. . . and carried it out of the sea and into the sky.

They sailed through the air, over sea and land. All the way back . . .

. . . to Grandude's garden!

One of the accordionship's windows creaked open . . .

"Hey, Nandude!"

Grandude and the Chillers waved,
as Nandude climbed down from the ship.

"Nandude to the rescue!" she said with a wink,
giving them all a big hug.

"Goodness me, you've all grown up so much." Nandude sounded
a bit worried. "I must have been away far longer than I thought!"

"After all that, I think it's time
for some tea and biscuits," said Grandude.

As they got cosy in the living room,
Nandude told them all about her adventures.

And then it was time for bed. Nandude played lullabies on her accordion while the Chillers snuggled down.

"Maybe we can go on an adventure with you, Nandude," Tom said with a yawn.

"Yes, maybe we can do that someday," she whispered. "That would be fun! Now, off to sleep you go."

Nandude and Grandude kissed the Chillers goodnight
and pretty soon they were fast asleep.

Nandude turned and smiled at Grandude –
but he was asleep too!

Sleep tight, Chillers.
Sleep tight, Grandude.